Early Impressions of Washington
PO Box 34
Hardinsburg IN 47125
(812)472-9494

ABC Yummy

Lisa Jahn-Clough

HOUGHTON MIFFLIN COMPANY BOSTON

1997

for Eric

Library of Congress Cataloging-in-Publication Data

Jahn-Clough, Lisa.
    ABC yummy / Lisa Jahn-Clough.
        p. cm.
    Summary: An alphabetical tour of good things to eat, from Alicia's
appetizing asparagus to Zoe's zesty zucchini.
    ISBN 0395-84542-4 (hardcover)
    [1. Food—Fiction. 2. Alphabet.]   I. Title
PZ7.J153536Abd 1997
[E]—dc20   98-27755
                                                                CIP
                                                                 AC

Walter Lorraine (wx) Books

All rights reserved. For information about permission
to reproduce selections from this book, write to Permissions,
Houghton Mifflin Company, 215 Park Avenue South,
New York, New York 10003.
For information about this and other Houghton Mifflin trade
and reference books and multimedia products, visit The Bookstore
at Houghton Mifflin on the World Wide Web at
http://www.hmco.com/trade/.

Printed in Singapore
TWP   10   9   8   7   6   5   4   3   2   1

ALICIA'S APPETIZING

ASPARAGUS

DANDELIONS

DAPHNE'S DELICIOUS

ELENA'S ENORMOUS EGGPLANT

FRANKIE'S FABULOUS FIG

GEORGE'S GORGEOUS

GRAPEFRUIT

ISABELLE'S IRRESISTIBLE ICEBERG LETTUCE

JEFF, JESS AND JIM'S JUICY JAM

KYLE'S

KISSABLE KIWI

MONUMENTAL MUSHROOM

MATT AND MARTY'S

NICKI AND NATE'S NUTRITIOUS NECTARINE

OLIVER'S

OUTRAGEOUS OLIVE

QUENTIN'S

QUENCHING QUINCE

RANDY'S RADIANT RADISH

SOPHIE'S SUCCULENT STRAWBERRY

TASTY TOMATO

VINCE, VIC AND VAL'S

VARIED VEGETABLES

WALTER'S

WACKY WATERMELON

YUMMY YAM

YOLANDA AND YVONNE'S

ZOE'S ZESTY ZUCCHINI

Aa Bb Cc
Dd Ee Ff
Gg Hh Ii Jj
Kk Ll Mm

The End